The Funny Cat Adventure

They lived in a small house
with their parents.

One day, a funny cat
came to their door.

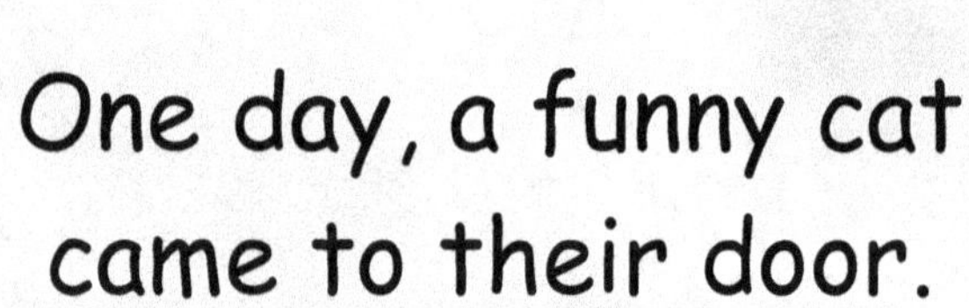

The cat had big, round eyes.

It wore a tiny, red hat.

"Can we keep it?"
asked Dhonthi.

Ali smiled and said,
"Yes, please!"

The cat meowed loudly.

It jumped into the house.

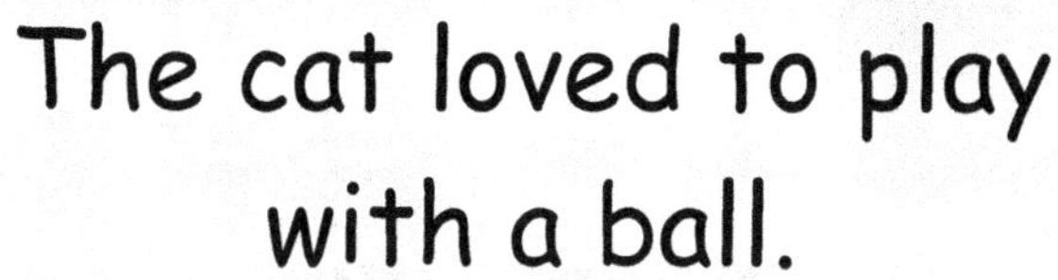

The cat loved to play
with a ball.

Ali threw the ball.

The cat ran fast to catch it.

Dhonthi laughed,
"It's so funny!"

The cat did a little dance.

It spun around on its tail.

Ali clapped his hands.

Dhonthi joined in the fun.

The cat liked to jump
on the sofa.

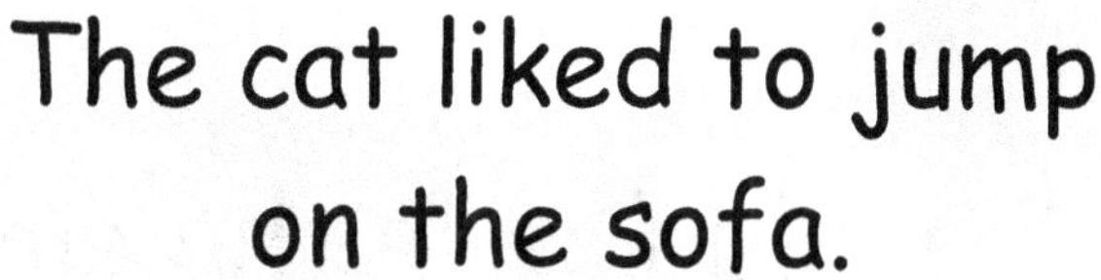

It would flip in the air!

"Wow!" said Ali.

"Look at it go!" Dhonthi said.

The cat was always hungry.

It ate lots of fish.

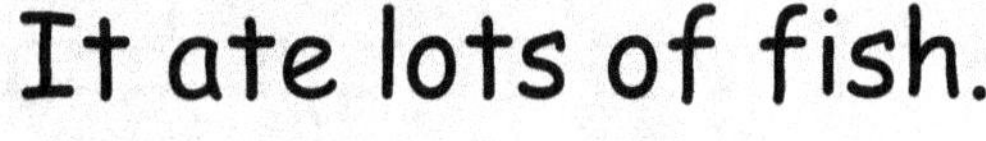

Ali gave it some milk.

Dhonthi gave it a small cookie.

The cat purred and
rubbed their legs.

At night, the cat
liked to cuddle.

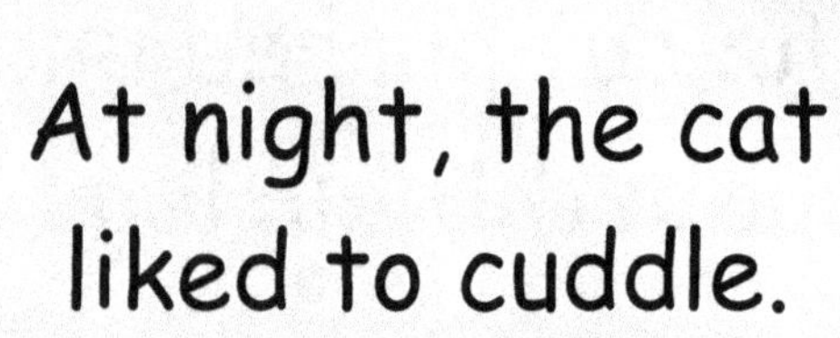

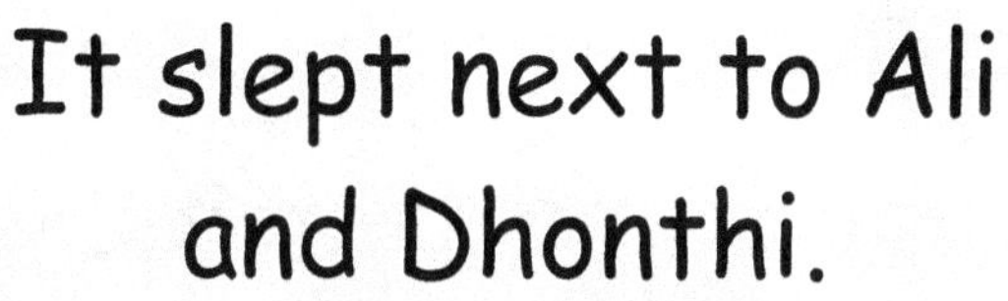

It slept next to Ali
and Dhonthi.

They told the cat
bedtime stories.

The cat listened carefully.

One day, the cat went on an adventure.

It ran to the park.

Ali and Dhonthi followed it.

The cat climbed a tall tree.

"Come down!" Dhonthi called.

But the cat was brave.

It jumped down safely.

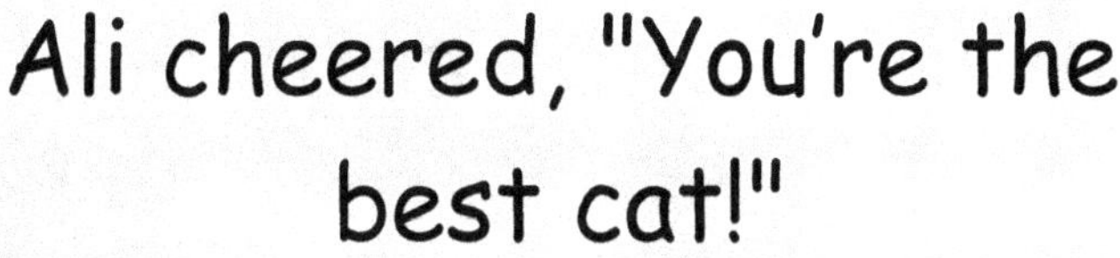

Ali cheered, "You're the best cat!"

Dhonthi gave the cat a big hug.

The funny cat loved to explore.

It chased butterflies in the garden.

It jumped over puddles.

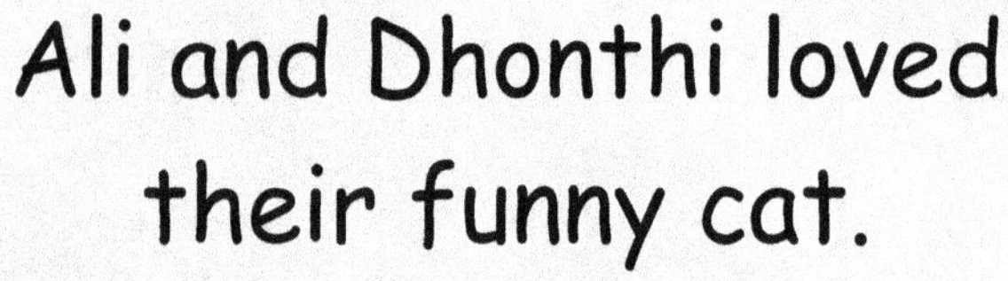

Ali and Dhonthi loved
their funny cat.

The cat was their best friend.

Every day was fun
with the cat.

They went on many
adventures.

They played hide and seek.

The cat always found them!

Sometimes, the cat hid too.

Ali and Dhonthi searched everywhere.

They found it under the bed.

"Gotcha!" said Dhonthi.

The cat meowed happily.

It loved to play all day.

Ali and Dhonthi were
never bored.

Their cat was always there.

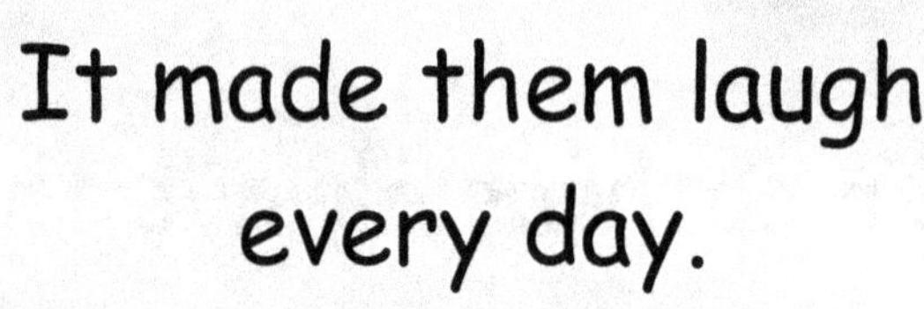

It made them laugh
every day.

The funny cat was so special.

Ali and Dhonthi took
care of it.

They fed it, played with it, and loved it.

The cat loved them back.

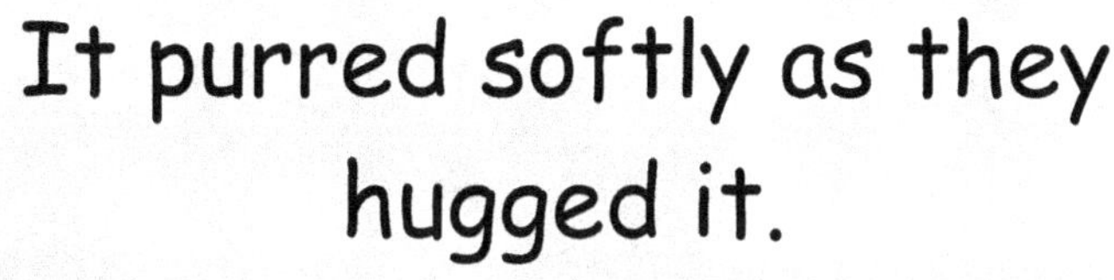

It purred softly as they
hugged it.

Ali said, "Our cat is the best."

Dhonthi agreed, "It's the funniest cat ever!"

And they all lived happily ever after.

The End.